This Yael book belongs to:

....

New Shoes for Yael

Published by Lite Girl Inc.

1st Edition, August 2012
2nd Edition, June, 2014

Credits:
Illustrations and book design: Steve Pileggi/Blue Lion Designs
Cover Design: Goldy Mermelstein
Editorial Direction: Tzippy Caton

Music and lyrics:
Mattisyahu Brown
Vocalist: Rachel Ravitz
Audio Recording and production: Rochel Leah Reifer

Summary: Yael, Lite Girl's original lovable character, learns that everyone's perfect in their own way.

Library of Congress Cataloging—VA 1-776-193

Printed In China

ISBN 978-0-9835231-4-7-51699

עוז והדר לבושה ותשחק ליום אחרון

This book is dedicated in loving memory
Of our unforgettable

Mother, Grandmother and Great Grandmother

Mrs. Genendl Bas Rav Shlomo Berkowitz zt'l

Whose attributes, bravery, contentment, diligence, devotion, exertions, frugality,
gentleness, humaneness, love ,intelligence, modesty, perseverance, quiet demeanor,
righteousness, simplicity, sincerity, tenacity, uniqueness, work ethic and wisdom

Continues to inspire, motivate and energize our lives as we endeavor to walk in her
balanced path of דרך הממוצע

אשר היא דרך הישרה והיא דרך החכמים (רמב״ם הל׳ דעות:א)
עשות משפט ואהבת חסד והצנע לכת עם אלקך (מיכה ו:ח)

Avrohom Pinchas and Mindy Berkowitz., children & grandchildren עמו״ש

Summer was ending in a few more days,
Yael was excited to start Pre-1A!
She had new crayons, a backpack too,
But Yael still needed a new pair of shoes.

Sunday Morning was a beautiful day,
Mommy and Yael were on their way.
Patiently they waited at the bus stop,
For a bus to take them to the shoe shop!

Waiting to be fitted, Yael watched the busy store—
So many children and shoes on the floor!
All of them seemed to be having fun,
Only Yael seemed nervous as she watched everyone.

The Salesman showed Yael purple shoes
and pink shoes and mary janes in red,
He showed her many other pairs
But she only shook her head!

Mommy and the Salesman kept on trying,
They brought out many pairs;
But Yael didn't like any—
And she left the store in tears.

They visited another store,
They brought enough shoes to make a mess!
Yael looked at every one
But she just couldn't say "yes"!

It was getting very late,
Other children had new shoes in their bags.
Only Yael went home empty-handed
Looking very sad.

What's the matter, Yael?" Mommy asked
later.
"Why do you seem so upset?"
"We'll look some more, tomorrow,
We'll find you school shoes yet!"

Yael thought about the shoes
She wanted to be getting—
HIGH Heeled ones like Mommy wore
To her cousin's wedding!

She thought of all the tall ladies,
Dancing to the music's beat—
And the high, high heels
On all their feet.

You see, Yael was already five
But she wasn't very tall;
Some people thought she still was four
Because she still looked very small!

Savta said she was "Teeny Weeny",
Great Aunt Bracha called her "Itsy-Bitsy"!
Her brother David said she was short.
But she wanted to be tall and pretty!

So Yael had tried on Mommy's heels,
She marched down the hall,
She looked in the mirror,
YES! Now she was tall!

Yael explained all this to her Mother—
How she liked to feel so high
"But none of the shoes we saw today had heels!"
She said with a sigh.

Mommy called to Abba,
  Who arrived with a twinkle in his eyes.
"Did you know my dear Yael,
  That Hashem made you the perfect size?"

"He measured you so carefully,
  And chooses just how fast you'll grow—
Because he has special jobs
  For all of us you know!"

"David may be very good reaching things
From high places.
But you're better at playing hide and seek,
Cause you fit into small spaces!"

Yael remembered how she'd had the best
Hiding place of all her friends;
No one could find her
And she'd won in the end!

"It doesn't matter if you're petite or tall
Hashem loves you this way best of all!"

"And for me, Yael, you're the perfect size,
Because you fit nice and snug
When I put my arms around you
And twirl you in a hug!"

Yael felt much better!
It was nice to know
Hashem made her just right.
She stood in front of Mommy's mirror,
And agreed she was the perfect height.

So Yael got new school shoes, perfect for Pre-1a.
She showed them off so proudly; it was a happy
day!

Hashem made each of us perfectly,
Yael thought, smiling from ear to ear.
She loved her new shoes, and Hashem loved her—

It was going to be a wonderful year!

PLACE HEEL
HERE

lite girl's
shoe size chart

Inches 3 0

1

2 Sizes

Inches 4 3

4

5

Inches 5 6

7 Sizes

8

Inches 6 9

10

11

Inches 7 12 Sizes

13

1

Inches 8 2

3

4

Inches 9 5

From your head to your toes, you're perfect the way you are!

Here's the Hello World song lyrics. Hope you'll sing along!
And remember, you can be a Lite Girl too!

(You can listen to the song being played on the *New Shoes for Yael* CD)

Hello, World, Hello, here I am!
I want you to know that I'm happy to be me
And I'm happy to be just the way I am

Hashem made me perfectly from my head to my toes
Because Hashem loves me and because He knows—
That it's right for me to be exactly who I am
And I'm so happy this is the 'me' that He chose-

Short or tall; big or small
Every LITE Girl knows
We're perfect the way we are!
So say 'hello' to the whole wide world with a brilliant smile
Because you know you are Hashem's Shining Star!

Hello World, Hello, here I am!
Hello Whole Wide World, Hello, here I am!
I want you to know that I'm happy to be me
And I'm happy to be just the way I am...

Just the way I am...
Just the way I am...
Hashem made me perfectly
Just the way I am...

Oh, Oh. Oh......